TO:

FROM:

Jesus said, "Let the little children come to me,
and do not hinder them, for the Kingdom of Heaven
belongs to such as these."

WHY THE WORLD NEEDS THIS BOOK SERIES

Welcome to the playful and endearing adventures of Church Dog. Each story uses biblical foundations to teach moral lessons about real life issues that children face. While the books have Christian underpinnings, they promote universal values. The books are perfect for igniting conversations around subjects like bullying, grief, prejudice, forgiveness, fear and fighting temptation. Equally important is stressing the power of being kind, compassionate, giving, standing up for one other and having self-esteem.

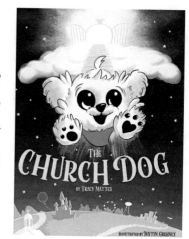

The Church Dog series invites children of all ages to look at themselves and others through the eyes of a loving God, as true princes & princesses of Heaven. Come along on the journey and find yourself on the pages of these relatable books, which are sure to become favorites your children will want to read again and again.

In this second Church Dog adventure, when the whole world goes into hiding from a scary germ, K'noot and his furry friends decide to play the hero and hunt down the pesky bug. But sniffing for what they imagine to be a giant monster sends them on the wrong mission. They quickly learn that even a Big Bad Bug is no match for Jesus, who squashes all fears!

ACKNOWLEDGMENTS

As creator and author of the Church Dog series, I cannot express enough appreciation to my Church Dog partners for their amazing contributions, continued support and encouragement. A special thanks to Justin Greenly, Illustrator; Rev. Dr. William Lewis, Spiritual Director, series development and editor; Michele Lewis, contributing writer, editor and story development; and Kim Hawk, public relations, social media and product management. I also offer my sincere gratitude for our consultants, Elijah Lewis in creative directing and Rod Hawk for professional photography, Web and CRM consulting.

To my sweet Maltese dog, the real K'noot, who inspired this story.

My heartfelt thanks to these people and so many others, without whose support the completion of this project could not have been accomplished.

Finally, to our Lord Jesus Christ, the One and Only, who went to the cross so that we could tell His story of love to children of all generations. All credit for this project goes to the Author and Creator of Life, Almighty God.

Church Dog and the Big Bad Bug
Copyright © 2021 by Tracy Mattes

First Printing 2021

ISBN: 9781087857060

CHURCH DOG &
THE BIG, BAD BUG

BY TRACY MATTES

ILLUSTRATIONS BY JUSTIN GREENLY

TABLE OF CONTENTS

CHAPTER 1
BAD NEWS

K'noot was resting on a cushion near the window in Pastor William's office when he heard the door open abruptly.

A man rushed in and handed him a paper. As Pastor
read, K'noot noticed a look on his face he had never
seen before.

Still holding the paper, Pastor slowly sat back in his chair. It looked like he was carrying the weight of the world on his shoulders.

A loud ring interrupted his troubled stare. Pastor answered. The voice on the speakerphone sounded panicked. "This is getting really bad. All the churches in town are closing their doors and going online only. I've prayed hard about this and it looks like we're going to have to close our church too. I'll call you back."

K'noot's ears perked and his head shot straight up. CLOSE THE CHURCH? That's crazy!

K'noot trotted over to Pastor William, who was now sitting with both hands on his head. The worried pup jumped up on the desk and nudged his downcast friend with a cold, wet nose. Pastor looked up at K'noot and gave him a comforting pat.

"Oh K'noot, we're going to have to close the church to protect our people from this mysterious virus."

K'noot's eyes grew large and he backed up two puppy steps.

"But… but…PASTOR! We can't close the church!" His upset whimpers landed on human ears that couldn't understand him. "If you want to save people you don't close the church, you open the church. You know this! I'm only the Church Dog and even I know this."

K'noot loved Pastor William's big heart. Despite the deep sadness in his eyes he was willing to do something he clearly didn't want to do, because he loved the people at his church. He had the heart of Jesus.

The office door swung open and two people walked in looking very somber. "We need to make a decision Pastor."

This was really happening. Everything seemed to be spinning for K'noot. Even though he knew it was necessary, the thought of closing the church was more than his little puppy heart could handle. What could he do to help? He wished he was back in Heaven to ask Jesus what to do. K'noot was so upset, he somehow forgot that Jesus was always with him, just a prayer away.

Pastor's words kept repeating in K'noot's head, over and over. "People are getting very sick from this nasty bug."

What kind of bug is this? K'noot pondered as he paced back and forth. If this nasty bug was the reason people were getting sick, then maybe he could find it and squash it before the big, bad bug hurt anybody else! Then the church could open again!

"It's probably like a big flea." K'noot scratched, just imagining the itchy pests in his fur. Then again, he had never heard of anyone pushing up daisies from catching fleas.

No, this must be bigger. K'noot pictured a giant 10-foot-tall, poisonous, creepy crawly critter. He gulped. But then he remembered the Bible story of David fighting Goliath and took courage.

If a small boy could defeat a ferocious giant to save God's people, then a little dog could beat a ferocious giant bug. K'noot imagined himself a hero, reopening the church for God's people!

CHAPTER 3
GETTING HELP

K'noot was ready to go into battle, but he needed some back up. He knew just the dog he could rely on for help. His ol' buddy Shep, a former military dog who won all sorts of cool medals. Shep was the wisest dog K'noot had ever met. All the neighborhood dogs looked up to him.

K'noot snuck out of his doggy door and ran down the street
to a big, white house with giant porches and a red door.
It was a short distance from Tracy's condo, where K'noot
lived. The back yard of Shep's home was enclosed by a
huge fence that backed up to a dog park.

K'noot wiggled his little body under the fence and made a b-line to Shep, who was resting under the shade of his big back porch. Shep saw K'noot running towards him.

"Hey K'noot!" He barked. "How ya doin' ol' pal?"

"Shep, Shep! I need… your…help!" K'noot panted. He was so out of breath he almost collapsed. "We have a big problem."

"Settle down, little dude. What's going on?"

"There's a giant bu.. bu.. bug out there."

"What are you talking about?" Shep barked. "What kind of bug?"

"I don't know but it's making people 'sick as a dog,' or worse." K'noot's voice cracked. "It could hurt the humans we love if we don't stop it."

"Hmm. Now that you mention it, my humans have been acting odd lately… I mean," Shep pawed at the bandana covering his snout, "Look at me."

"Is that a dog muzzle?" K'noot cocked his head, puzzled.

"Yup! Even our humans are starting to wear them now. And they're buying truckloads of toilet paper and using words like 'social distancing' and 'quarantine' a lot."

Just then, a tiny brown hamster named Chester came rolling past them in his clear plastic ball. "I don't understand what the big deal is about quarantine! I spend most of my time in a plastic bubble. Now, everybody wants to be Chester! I could make a fortune on this thing!"

K'noot and Shep were distracted for a moment watching Chester roll his clear ball right by them and off the edge of the porch. It landed with a loud THUMP!

"You alright, little guy?" Shep barked.

"Still working out a few kinks!" Chester squeaked, seeing stars as he bounced a few feet. Then he kept on cruising, singing the tune "rolllin'...rollin'...rollin'..."

"You've gotta help me find this bug and stomp it out, Shep!"
K'noot continued. "They've closed the church!"

"Closed the church!" Shep jumped back in surprise.
"Good golly! This IS an emergency. We're going to need all
the dogs on this case."

With that, Shep let out his loudest alert howl. Four legged
friends of all sizes came running from every direction.
"We're here for you, little friend," he said, as dogs
gathered around him.

CHAPTER 4
WHAT IS IT?

"What's going on?" Dogs of all sizes woofed and howled. K'noot was comforted to see so many familiar faces.

Shep addressed the pack like a general, barking orders. "Alright everyone, listen up! We have a very serious situation here. Some sort of dangerous bug is on the loose. It's biting and stinging our humans. We need to come up with a plan to stop it."

"Yes." K'noot panted, urgently. "We don't have much time."

"Well then, better tell us everything you know about this bug, starting with its name."

"It's, it's… oh, it's a big word that starts with a "C." K'noot tried to remember.

"Centipede?"
One dog woofed.

"No."

"Cricket?"

"No."

"Cockroach!" Shep barked.
"It has to be a cockroach.
Those suckers are nasty."

"Uh, uh." K'noot
shook his head.

"Caterpillar?"
Another panted eagerly.

"No."

"Stink Bug?" A little dog yapped.

"That doesn't start with a 'C,'"
Shep growled.

"Could be a soft 'C.'"

"Yeah, it's those silent
but deadly ones to watch out for.
Hee hee hee," Another dog
snickered.

"I remember now!" A name came back to K'noot. "C. Rona!"

"Never heard of any bug by that name 'round here," Shep said looking doubtful.

The other dogs shared puzzled looks, then shrugged. "Where does it come from?"

"Maybe C. Rona hitched a ride here on a rat." A hound dog piped in. "Rats are known for carrying bugs."

"Oh, sure, accuse the rat! Such a stereotype!" Chester came rolling over in his plastic ball. "My people are blamed for everything!"

"What do you mean, YOUR people? You're a hamster." Goldie rolled her eyes while the other dogs chuckled.

"Well, my great, great grandfather was a rat. I'm descended from a long line of unfairly insulted rodents."

"You mean, super spreaders." Shep muttered under his breath.

"Oh!" Chester clutched his furry chest. "Unfair! So are bats!"

"Bats are just flying rats." Shep teased. "Got any of them in your family tree Chester?"

"I'm so confused." A sad looking Basset hound sighed, trying to picture Chester with wings and hanging upside down from a tree limb.

Together, all the dogs watched Chester roll away in his bubble yelling, "We shall overcome!"

"What's wrong with bats?" A little wiener dog stopped sniffing the ground for a snack. "Add a little BBQ sauce. Tastes like chicken!"

"Ick!" A posh, white poodle shivered. "That would make me sick."

"Exactly!" K'noot brought their attention back to their mission. "We don't know where this bug comes from. We just have to stop it from making our humans sick."

CHAPTER 5

BATTLE PLAN

"Okay, okay! I need everyone to focus now." Shep tried to redirect the conversation back to the task at hand. "Enough with the guessing games. Tell us everything you know about this big, bad bug, K'noot."

"This bug is a friend to no one in the world."
K'noot explained. "It's attacking
people all around the globe.
Now it's here. So, it's up to us to find
this bug and ZAP it!"

"That's right!" Shep said.
"We're the superheroes now.
The fate of the world is in our
paws."

"Oh, I know what I'm wearing! My
sparkle cape and mask," Goldie
whispered with giddy excitement to the
other dogs. "You can look glamorous
and still save the world."

There was a hushed moment as each dog
pictured themselves wearing the costume of
their favorite alter-ego.

"Ok, now every dog spread out!" Shep directed,
puffing out his chest as he imagined himself a caped
superhero. "Check under the house, the playground, the
garden, and all around the yard! Report back if you find any
mysterious bugs. If the culprit is here, we'll get it."

The dogs took off in every direction, sniffing the ground, turning over logs, digging through the flower beds and even crawling under the house.

His furry friends were on a mission to help the Church Dog find this big, bad bug.

CHAPTER 6
HEAVENLY VISIT

K'noot got busy inspecting the yard. Yet before his nose could track down a single bug, he was distracted by a mysterious sound. "K'nooooot."

"Hello?" The pup lifted one ear, looking around. "Did someone call my name?"

"Over here, K'noot." Came a distant reply. The voice was strangely familiar.

K'noot followed the sound to a small garden. He nudged the gate open and was soon walking past beautiful flowers and luscious trees. He stopped in front of a lovely pond to listen for the voice.

"Hello?" He barked out, a little frightened. "Is anybody here?"

Just then, he looked down into the clear water of the pond and saw the reflection of Jesus standing right beside him. K'noot's heart jumped for joy!

"Am I glad to see you!" K'noot instantly forgot all his fears and nuzzled his fuzzy head into best friend's hand.

"Walk with me," Jesus said. K'noot happily trotted by his Heavenly Master's side. After awhile Jesus said, "Look up K'noot."

"The Church Dog's eyes opened wide, suddenly aware of a dome shaped shield overhead. There where dangereous bugs with fangs falling like torpedos, but they could not get through God's protective forcefield.

"Whoaaa! I wish everyone could see what I see." The Heaven sent pup's supernatural eyes sparkled. "Then no one would be afraid, EVER!"

"I love your spirit, K'noot." Jesus smiled. "You have the courageous heart of David. While **your** special eyes can see the enemy, this bug is not an insect like a spider that your friends can find. In fact, it's so tiny, the human eye can't detect it. Even the best doctors need a special machine called a microscope to make it out."

K'noot's face dropped. "But Master. How can they fight it, if they can't even see it?"

"You fight this giant the same way David fought his," Jesus said, "With faith."

"What is faith?"

"Keeping your focus on Me. Trusting Me. Like David did when he stepped up to fight Goliath. The entire nation was afraid. Even the biggest and strongest men were trembling with fear because of the giant. They felt helpless."

"Like people today feel about this bug!" K'noot barked.

Jesus nodded. "But do you know why David wasn't scared, even though he was the smallest? Even though everyone else around him was terrified?"

CHAPTER 7
FIGHTING GIANTS

K'noot's eyes drew big in anticipation of the answer. "Faith?" He guessed.

"Yes," Jesus continued, "Because he didn't rely on his own strength to defeat the giant. David relied on God's power. I believe down here you kids call it "Superpower.""

"Wow! That's so cool! God has superpowers. Just like this shield."

"My Father is the King of Heaven's Armies," Jesus replied. "And this shield is only one of many Heavenly weapons available to His earthly children."

"Wow! Wait 'till Shep hears about this!" K'noot said. "Faith over Fear! That's how we will defeat this invisible bug!"

"That's right K'noot. People are scared. They need hope. This is a time they need to rely on Me to care for them. That's your mission. Tell people I love them and I'm fighting for them."

"Cool!" K'noot jumped up with joy. "You're the greatest superhero of all!"

"Do you want to see another superpower?" Jesus sat K'noot on His lap, the way he used to do in Heaven. With one finger, He opened the sky like a curtain in front of them to reveal captured moments in time. Together they watched several different scenes of families in their homes praying, reading the bible, or watching Pastor William's message of hope on their computers.

"The church may be closed, but you see, I live in the hearts of people. My love is not contained in any building or place. Pastor William understands this. His church will reopen soon. My Father made all people, young and old. He loves them all very much. And because He loves them, He takes extra good care of them. And their furry best friends, too."

K'noot looked thoughtful. "Then how come God is still letting people get sick?"

Jesus gazed at the pup with understanding eyes. "God created the world a perfect place with no suffering or sickness. But Adam and Eve chose to disobey God. When that happened, suffering and pain came into the world, like this virus. Now good things and bad things happen to everyone. But God's love for His children is bigger than their mistakes and He works everything out for their good. He doesn't always take the hard stuff away, but He brings you through it. He is always with you and He will never leave you, ever."

"That's great news!" K'noot jumped up. "So, we don't need to be afraid of anything, because God loves us and is always looking out for us!"

"That's right. You have the heart of a warrior, K'noot and so do your furry friends. Tell them what I said. Ask them to join you in spreading this message of hope. It's what people need right now. Leave everything else up to Me. And at just the right time, I'll squash that bug." Jesus winked at K'noot.

Feeling so much better, K'noot ran back to find Shep.

"Hey, little dude, where've ya been?"

"I've been talking to Jesus, and I have some good news!"

"Well, spit' er out!"

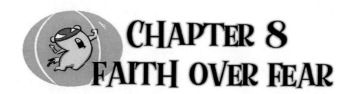

"This big, bad bug is no match for God! We don't have to worry at all, because God loves us. And our humans. He is always looking out for us. He's on our team!"

"Yeeaaahh great news! God's our coach! So what's our next play?"

"Well, for now we can all do things like keep our paws clean, wear masks and social distance. Chester you can give us some tips on that. This will help keep everyone safe. But we don't have to live in fear. We need to put all of our faith in God, who protects us. We need to remember, God is bigger than any monster, bug or problem we face."

When K'noot finished telling all the other dogs everything Jesus had said, they cheered and praised their Holy Coach with loud barks and happy howls.

Later, as K'noot trotted home, he noticed Pastor William was still in his office. K'noot knew in his heart Pastor was worried.

"People are scared." K'noot remembered the words of Jesus. The little pup needed to find a way to share Jesus' good news with his human friend. He decided to make a detour.

A minute later, the Church Dog was jumping up on Pastor's desk.

"K'noot?" Pastor William practically fell out of his chair, then chuckled. "What brings you here, little fella?"

K'noot answered by ruffling a page of Pastor's Bible. Seeing the bewildered human frown, he thumped his little paw down on the open page.

Pastor started reading the passage aloud.

"Do not be afraid, for the LORD your God loves you and goes with you; He will never leave you. He will never forsake you."

DO NOT BE AFRAID

Pastor looked up at the Church Dog with understanding eyes. "Of course, K'noot! You clever little dog. If I didn't know better, I would think you actually know this Bible." He picked up the pup and hugged him. "This battle belongs to the Lord. Thank you for this reminder. It was just what I needed."

He sat down again and began flipping through the Bible with fresh hope. "This nasty bug may still be around, but Jesus is fighting our battles. Isn't that right, K'noot? We need to tell everyone not to be afraid, because God loves them and is always watching over them."

"Woof! Woof!" The Church Dog barked in agreement.

"We need to remind everyone that their Faith in God is powerful enough to push any of our Fears right off the cliff."

"Yes!" K'noot howled. "Faith over Fear!"

A Special Message to Parents

Dear Parent,

Thank you for welcoming "The Church Dog" into your home.

Faith begins at the ages of understanding. Like a tiny seed, it grows. Jesus has been my best friend all my life. For most of us on the Church Dog team, our close bond with God began as children during precious moments of story time with our parents and grandparents. I remember being fascinated hearing the stories about Jesus and how I was part of a bigger story— God's story. That promise they placed in our hearts as children, remains today. As this book is in your hands, you probably have the same desire for your little one to walk through life with the Creator of the Universe by their side. Can you think of anything better for your child?

The goal for the Church Dog book series is to ignite the hearts of children and open their eyes to a loving God who sees them as the beautiful, unique and special individuals they are.

In God's Grip,

Tracy Mattes
& the Church Dog Team

For More Church Dog Adventures
go to
www.churchdog.org

THE CHURCH DOG

The very first book of the Church Dog Series was released on November 1st 2020. The Church Dog is a heartwarming tale about a puppy sent from Heaven to teach people about the true nature of God's unconditional love. With supernatural eyes that let him see people the way Jesus does, the Church Dog's mission is to help God's children understand their true identity as precious, unique and special to God.

God loves us no matter what. What better messenger than "Man's best friend?

CHURCH DOG MEETS A MARSHMALLOW

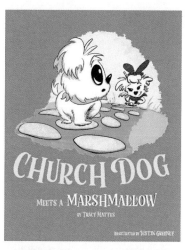

There are all sorts of things for a frisky puppy to discover when Tracy takes K'noot to visit a mysterious house next to the town Dog Park. He encounters new four-legged friends, a scary slobber-monster and a jaw dropping wonder.

Join the fun as the Church Dog catches sight of a walking vision that makes his heart melt like a marshmallow. You are sure to laugh at his comical, head-in-the-clouds infatuation and starry-eyed attempts to display his bravery as he crashes into a date with Destiny.

CHURCH DOG & THE INVISIBLE MAN

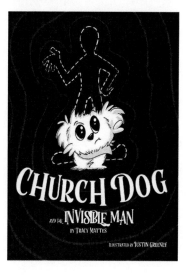

For the first time in his favorite place, K'noot sees something at Church that makes him sad. Using his heavenly superpower eyes, that see people the way Jesus does, he notices someone no-one else seems to be able to see.

Join the Church Dog as he uses his other worldly senses to draw people's attention back to what matters to God. Learn how the power of kindness and gentleness can restore the royal status and heavenly inheritance of anyone, even someone invisible.

About the Author

Tracy Mattes has been part of the Olympic Family for more than 25 years. Her passion has always been to share the values of sport with young children. Mattes was Director of Global Programs for the World Olympians Association and served in nine Olympic Games in various capacities within the organization. She also worked for sport National Governing Body Foundations, including seven years as Executive Director for the USA Water Ski & Wake Sports Foundation. As a competitive athlete, Mattes, a five-time All American, specialized in the 400-meter hurdles, ranking 7th in the world and was inducted into three Halls of Fame.

Mattes' career has taken her to more than 74 countries around the world. In 2005, she was selected as a United Nations Special Representative specializing in the advancement of young children through the values of education and sport. This unique global perspective comes through in her writing. She also has worked as a news producer and editor at three NBC affiliates. In 2010, Mattes won one of the top prizes at the 28th Milan International FICTS Film Festival for her documentary film "The Power of Education through Sport" which she produced, edited and narrated. For her efforts as a world class athlete and her humanitarian work, Mattes was honored by being inducted into the World Sport Humanitarian Hall of Fame in 2009.

She received her bachelor's degree in Broadcast Journalism from Arizona State University and her master's degree in International Business from the International University of Monaco in 2006 and was Valedictorian of her graduating class. Tracy has always shared her strong Christian faith throughout her career and she currently serves in a leadership position at Community Presbyterian Church in Celebration, Florida, the picturesque town that Disney built. Mattes lives there with her two Maltese dogs, K'noot and Marshmallow, who can hear the Church bells from their balcony.

Made in United States
North Haven, CT
06 December 2022

28026962R00031